INTO THE NIGHT

INTO THE NIGHT

BY DEBORAH HEILIGMAN
PICTURES BY MELISSA SWEET

HARPER & ROW, PUBLISHERS

Library of Congress Cataloging-in-Publication Data
Heiligman, Deborah.
Into the night / by Deborah Heiligman ; illustrations by Melissa
Sweet.
p.   cm.
Summary: A mother and son remember all the wonderful things they
did together that day as the little boy falls asleep for the night.
ISBN 0-06-026381-4 : $. — ISBN 0-06-026382-2 (lib. bdg.) :
$
[1. Mothers and sons—Fiction.   2. Bedtime—Fiction.   3. Stories
in rhyme.]   I. Sweet, Melissa, ill.   II. Title.
PZ8.3.H4132In   1990   89-24595
[E]—dc20   CIP
                                                                  AC

For my mother and my father
— DH

To Arno Werner
— MS

Into the night we go,
into the darkness,
steady and slow.

Over the trees
and through the stars,
and up to where
the night winds are.

The sky is waiting
for the moon—

Do you think our day
is over too soon?

We ran over the hills,
up to the sky,
and watched the bluebirds
and grackles fly.

We ran with the breeze
through the tall, wild grass
and picked daisies and violets
to put in a glass.

You found two big sticks
and four white stones.
I found a tree frog
and two pinecones.

We pushed each other
in an old tire swing,
and we listened to
an old man sing.

We ate pretzels and cheese
and drank lemonade.
Then we rested awhile
in the cool, quiet shade.

We sat in the sun
and told stories too.
You tickled me
and I tickled you.

Then we walked home
as the sun went down
and looked at the treasures
we had found.

It was a special day,
I know.

But now
into the night we go,
into the darkness,
steady and slow.

Let's look at the stars
and the bright, full moon.

It is time for night.
It is not too soon.